Peppa Pig™

Peppa's First Glasses

Peppa and George are outside playing with their friend Pedro Pony. They are busy jumping in muddy puddles. Splash! Splosh! Splish!
"Ha! Ha! Ha!" Peppa giggles as she jumps up and down.

Splosh!

Splash!

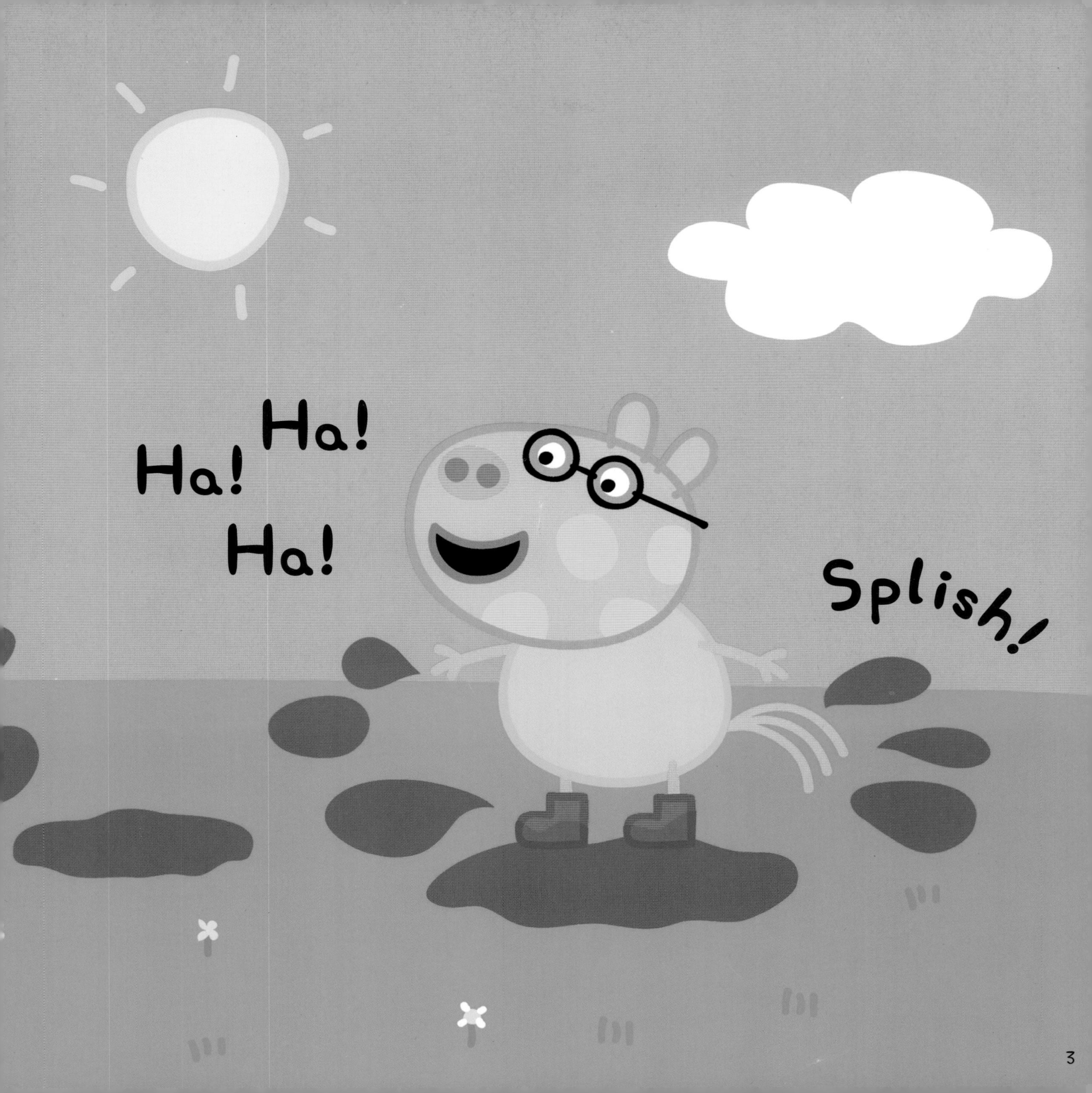
Ha! Ha!
Ha!
Splish!

"Argh! Ooh!" Pedro exclaims as he slips in a puddle and falls over. His glasses fly high into the air and land on the grass.

"Neigh! Where are my glasses?" Pedro asks Peppa and George, stumbling about. Pedro can't see very well without them.

Neigh!

Peppa and George look for Pedro's glasses. George quickly finds them and tries them on. "Silly George!" Peppa says. She takes the glasses and gives them back to Pedro. "Here they are." "Thank you," says Pedro as he puts them on.

"Pedro, why do you wear glasses?" Peppa asks.
"I need to," replies Pedro. "My daddy says so.
He's an optician."

"What's an optician?" Peppa wonders.
Pedro explains. "An optician checks that
you can see clearly. He does an eye test."

"Shall I give you an eye test?" Pedro asks Peppa.
Peppa agrees, and Pedro leans in close.

Snort!
Snort!

"Hmmm, interesting," he says, rubbing his chin.
"Close one eye and say what you can see."
"I can see George," Peppa says. George snorts.

"Now, close both eyes," Pedro instructs Peppa.
Peppa closes both her eyes.
"I can't see anything," Peppa says.
"Hmmm, can't see anything. Very, very
interesting . . ." Pedro says.
"I think you need glasses!"

Soon it is Pedro's home time. He waves goodbye to his friends and goes home with his mum.

Peppa and George go inside.
"Pedro gave me an eye test and I need
glasses," says Peppa. "When I closed
my eyes, I couldn't see anything."

"No one can see anything with their eyes closed," Mummy Pig explains.

"But . . ." Peppa sighs. ". . . Pedro knows all about glasses."
"All right, Peppa," chuckles Daddy Pig. "Let's take you to the optician for a proper eye test."

Peppa and Mummy Pig are at the optician's.
"What can I do for you?" Mr Pony asks Peppa.

"I need an eye test, please," Peppa replies, jumping up into his special chair.
"Of course," Mr Pony says. "Put these special glasses on and then look at the chart."
Mr Pony is going to test Peppa's eyes.

"Can you read these for me, please?" asks Mr Pony, pointing at some numbers.
Peppa says what she sees: "1, 2, 3, 4, 5, 6, 7, 8!"
"Very good," Mr Pony says.
"And now these colours, please."
"Red, orange, blue, green, yellow, purple!" says Peppa.
"Excellent!" Mr Pony says.

Mummy Pig helps Peppa try on some glasses
while Mr Pony checks the test results.
Some pairs look a little funny!

"How about these?" Mummy Pig says to Peppa holding
out some red, heart-shaped glasses.
"Wow! I like these ones, Mummy," says Peppa.
They both agree that Peppa looks fantastic in the glasses.

Mr Pony comes back with the results.
"Good news: Peppa has perfect eyesight!"
"Oh! So I don't need glasses." Peppa sighs disappointedly.
"But I really wanted some."

"Oh," Mr Pony says, thinking. "I suppose you
could have some sunglasses."
Peppa puts on a pair of red, heart-shaped sunglasses.
"Fantastic!" Peppa says. "I hope it's sunny every
day so I can always wear them!"

23

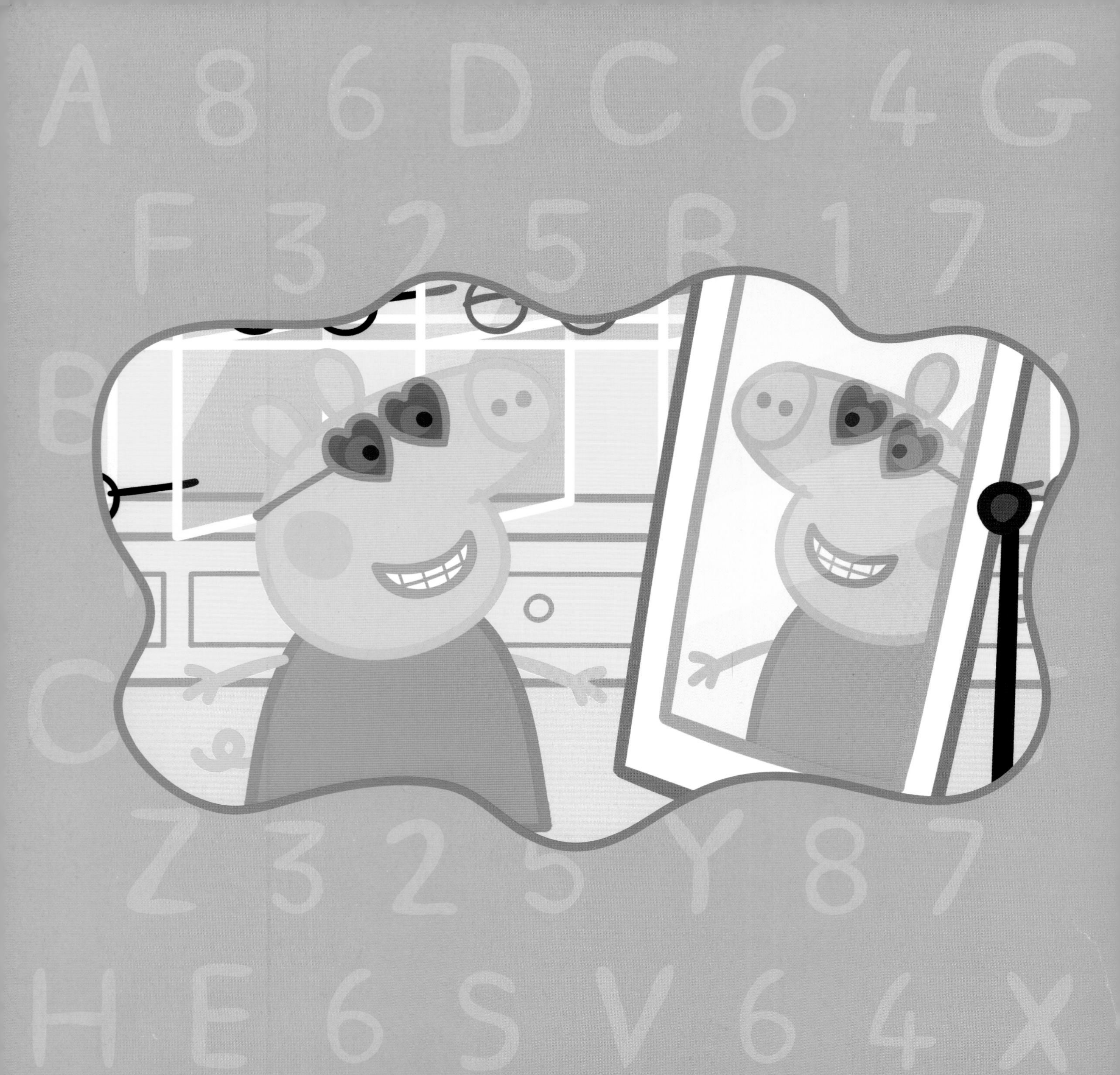

George Catches a Cold

Mummy Pig has said Peppa and George can play in the rain, but they must wear rain clothes to keep them dry.

But George hates wearing his rain hat,
so he has thrown it in a muddy puddle.

Hee, hee!

George!
Grunt!

"Come inside, children," calls Daddy Pig.

"It's raining very hard, now."

"Where's your hat, George?"

asks Mummy Pig.

"Atchoo!" replies George.

Oh dear. George has caught a cold.

"AAAATCHOOOOO!"

George cannot stop sneezing.

"Poor little George," says
Mummy Pig. "You don't look very well."
"Grunt. I'll call Doctor Brown-Bear,"
says Daddy Pig.

"Will George go to hospital?" asks Peppa.
"No, George has to go to bed," replies Daddy.
"So George is not properly ill then,"
says Peppa, disappointed.

"George, you have to stay in bed until you are better," says Daddy Pig.

"Why?" asks George.

"Because you have to keep warm," says Daddy.

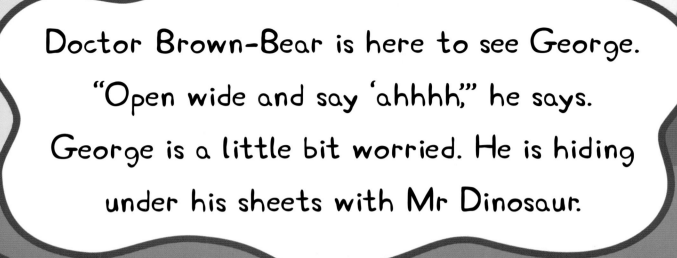

Doctor Brown-Bear is here to see George. "Open wide and say 'ahhhh,'" he says. George is a little bit worried. He is hiding under his sheets with Mr Dinosaur.

George finally comes out from under his sheets and opens his mouth wide for Doctor Brown-Bear to have a look inside. "Ahhhhhhh!"

"George has caught a cold," says Doctor Brown-Bear. "He can have some warm milk at bedtime, to help him sleep."
"Thank you Doctor Brown-Bear!" says Mummy Pig.

"You're welcome. Goodbye!" says
Doctor Brown-Bear, before driving off
in his special white car.

The next morning, George wakes up early.
The warm milk made him sleep very well.
"Roar!" cries George. He is feeling much better.

Roar!

It's a lovely sunny day but George is wearing his rain hat. He doesn't want to catch another cold.

Hee, hee, hee!

"Oh, George!
You don't need to wear your
hat when it is warm and sunny!"
Mummy Pig tells him.

"Hee, hee, hee!" everyone laughs.

Peppa Pig

Dentist Trip

Every morning, Peppa and George brush their teeth. Scrub! Scrub! Scrub!

51

"George, are your teeth
as clean as mine?"
Peppa asks, showing off
her clean white teeth.

"You both have lovely clean teeth.
I'm sure the dentist will be happy!"
calls out Daddy Pig.

Later that day, Peppa and George are at the dentist's, waiting for their check-up. It is George's first visit.

"Peppa! George! The dentist will see you now!" says Miss Rabbit, the nurse. "Hooray!" they both cheer.

This is Doctor Elephant, the dentist.
"Who's first?" he asks.

"I'm first," replies Peppa. "I'm a big girl.
Watch me, George!"

"Open wide, please!" orders
Doctor Elephant, softly.
"Aaaaah . . ." Peppa opens her mouth
as wide as she possibly can.
"Let's take a look!" says the dentist,
checking Peppa's teeth with a mirror.

"There. All done! What lovely clean teeth!" cheers Doctor Elephant. "Now you can have the special drink." Gargle! Ptooou! Peppa spits the pink liquid out into the sink. It's George's turn next.

George does not want it to be his turn.
So the dentist lets him hold Mr Dinosaur.
"All done. You have very strong, clean
teeth, George!" smiles Doctor Elephant.

"But wait, what is this?" cries Doctor Elephant. "George has clean teeth, but this young dinosaur's teeth are very dirty."

"The water jet, please, Miss Rabbit!" orders the dentist.
He uses the water to clean Mr Dinosaur's teeth.

Slosh!
Slosh!
Slosh!

"Pink!" cries George, picking up a glass. "That's right, George!" says the dentist. "Mr Dinosaur needs some special pink drink!" Gurgle! Gurgle!

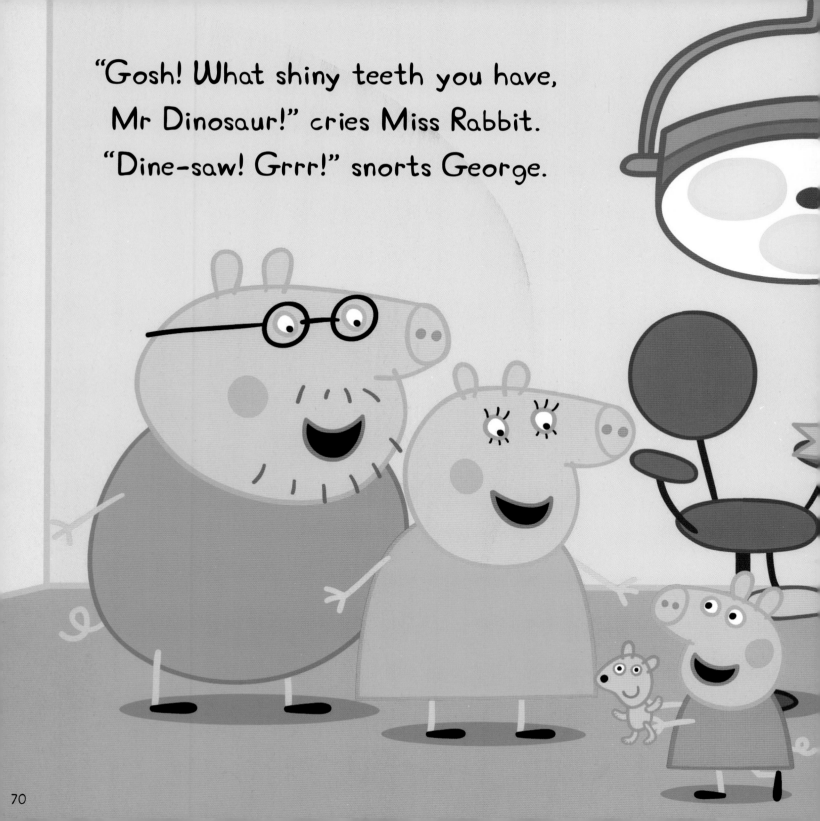

"Gosh! What shiny teeth you have,
Mr Dinosaur!" cries Miss Rabbit.
"Dine-saw! Grrr!" snorts George.

George loves Mr Dinosaur.
Especially now that he has
nice clean teeth.

Peppa Pig™

Nature Trail

Peppa and her family are going on a
nature trail. Mummy Pig asks
Daddy Pig not to forget the picnic.
"As if I would," laughs Daddy Pig.

They head off along the trail with their map.
Oh dear! Daddy Pig has left the picnic in the car.

Mummy and Daddy Pig ask Peppa if she can
see anything interesting in the forest.
"I don't see anything but boring trees," says Peppa.
Then she looks really hard and
finds some footprints on the ground.

"Let's follow the footprints and see who made them," says Mummy Pig.

"We will have to be very quiet so we don't scare anything away. Shhhh!"

Peppa and George follow the footprints along the ground.
"It looks like they were made by a little bird," says Mummy Pig.

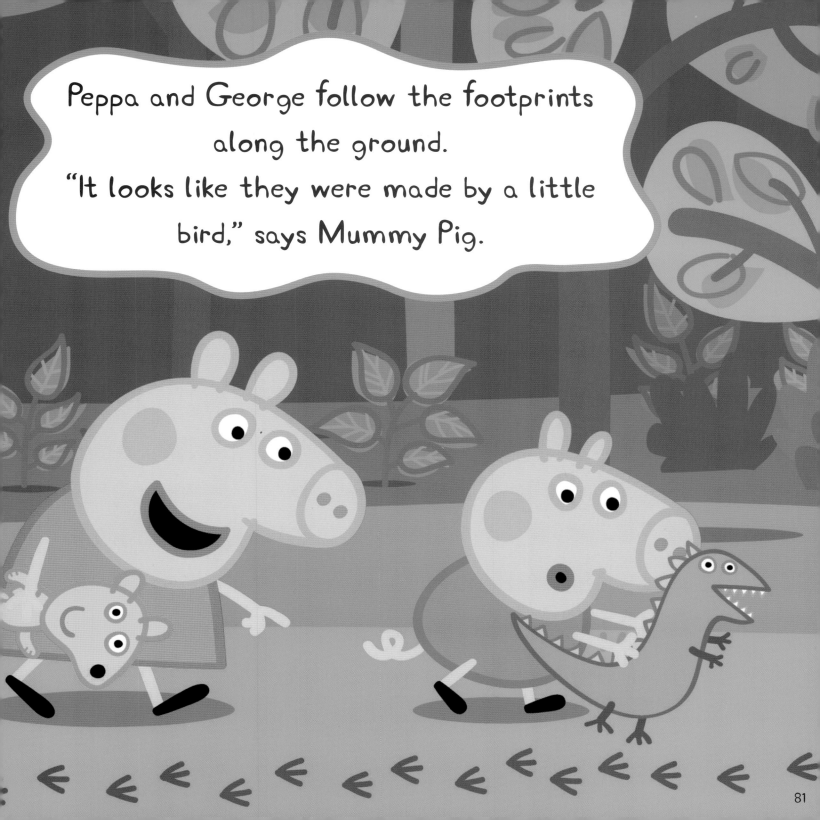

Soon, they come to the
end of the footprints.
"The bird has flown up into
that tree," smiles Daddy Pig.

"Where?" asks Peppa.
Daddy Pig gives Peppa binoculars
to help her see the bird.

83

George finds some more footprints.
They are very little. Daddy Pig says they
belong to ants collecting leaves to eat.

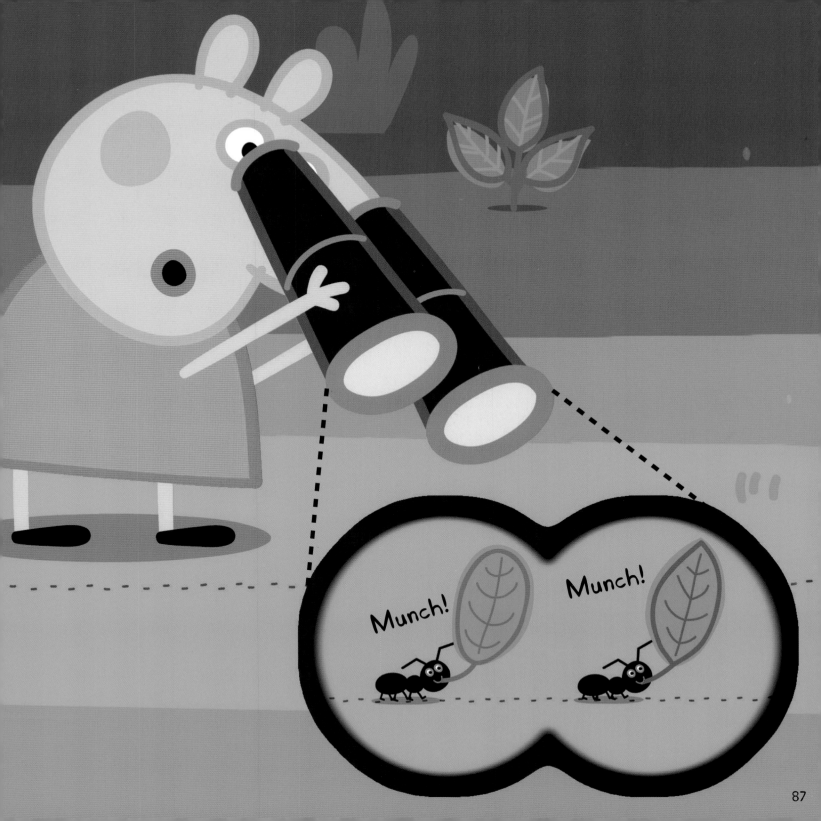

"I think it's time for lunch," says Mummy Pig. But Daddy Pig has left the picnic in the car!

"My map is wrong," begins Daddy Pig.
"We'll have to follow our own
footprints back to the car."

Suddenly, it starts to rain. It washes everyone's footprints away!
"How are we going to find the car, now?" asks Mummy Pig.

Quack! Quack!

"Ducks love picnics," says Peppa. "Mrs Duck, can you help us find our picnic please?"

The ducks lead Peppa and her
family back to their car.

"We're here! Thank you for your
help, Mrs Duck," cries Peppa.

"I love picnics!" laughs Daddy Pig.
The ducks love picnics too.
Quack! Quack! So do the birds!

And so do the ants!
Munch! Munch!
"Everybody loves picnics!" cries Peppa.

School Bus Trip

Peppa and her friends are
going on a school bus trip.

Woof!

"Let's check you are all here,"
says Madame Gazelle.
"Here!" cries Peppa.

Baaa! Grunt! Snort!

99

"Today," begins Madame Gazelle, "we are going on a trip to the mountains!"

"Hooray!"
cheer all the children.

Peppa and Suzy are
already a little hungry.
"Please can we eat our lunch now?"
they ask Madame Gazelle.

"Why not eat your apples and save the rest for the picnic?" she replies. Crunch! Crunch!

The bus has arrived at the foot of the mountain. The road is very steep! "Come on, bus! You can make it!" everyone cheers.

Peppa and her friends have finally made it
to the top of the mountain.
"Look at the view!" gasps Madame Gazelle.
All the children look out over the valley.

"Wow!" sighs Peppa, loudly.
"Wow! Wow! Wow!" Peppa hears
in the distance.
"What was that?" she asks quietly.
"It's your echo, Peppa!"
replies Madame Gazelle.

"An echo is the sound you hear when you speak loudly in the mountains," explains Madame Gazelle.
Grunt! Woof! Baaa! Snort!

Snort!

Grunt! Baaa!

Woof!

Now it's time for a picnic lunch.
Peppa loves picnics. Everyone loves
picnics! Munch! Slurp! Munch!
Yum! Yum!

"Where are the ducks?" asks Peppa, taking a bite of her sandwich. "They always turn up when we have picnics."

Quack! Quack! Quack!
Here come the ducks.

"Hello! Would you like some bread?"
Peppa asks them. The ducks are very lucky today.
There is plenty of bread!

The bus has arrived.
It's time to go home.

"Let's all sing a song!" suggests
Madame Gazelle. Hooray!
Everyone has had a great day!

119

Peppa Plays Football

It's a sunny day and Peppa Pig and
Suzy Sheep are playing tennis.
"To you, Suzy!" cheers Peppa, hitting
the ball. Now it's Suzy's turn.
"To you, Peppa!" she cries, hitting the ball
straight over Peppa's head. Oh dear!

"Waaaa!" George feels a bit left out.
"Sorry, George," says Peppa. "You can't play
tennis. We only have two racquets."
"George can be the ball boy!" cheers Suzy.
"Being a ball boy is a very important job,
George," says Peppa.

Peppa and Suzy are having lots of fun,
but they keep missing the ball.
"Ball boy!" they shout together.
"Huff, puff!" George is not having fun.
He keeps running to get the ball and
he is very tired!

"Hello, everyone," cries Peppa when her friends arrive. "We're playing tennis." "Can we play too?" asks Danny Dog. "There aren't enough racquets," replies Suzy Sheep.

"Let's play football then,"
says Danny Dog.
"Football! Hooray!"
everyone cheers.

"We can play girls against boys," says Peppa.
"Each team needs a goalkeeper," says Danny Dog.
"Me, me!" shouts Pedro Pony.
"Me, me!" cries Rebecca Rabbit.

Pedro Pony and Rebecca Rabbit
decide to be the goalkeepers.
"The boys' team will start!" says Danny Dog.
Richard Rabbit gets the ball and runs
very fast, right by Peppa Pig,
Suzy Sheep and Candy Cat
and straight up to the . . .

. . . "GOAL!" cry Danny and Pedro together, as Richard Rabbit kicks the ball straight past Rebecca Rabbit and into the net. "The boy is a winner!" cheers Danny Dog. "That's not fair, we weren't ready," moans Peppa.

Rebecca Rabbit picks up the ball and runs.

"Hey!" shouts Danny Dog.

"That's cheating! You can't hold the ball."

"Yes I can!" says Rebecca. "I'm the goalkeeper."

Rebecca throws the ball into the goal,

straight past Pedro Pony.

"GOAL!" she cries.

"That goal is not allowed," says Pedro.

"Yes, it is," says Peppa.

"No, it isn't!" barks Danny.

"What a lot of noise," snorts Daddy Pig.

"I'll be the referee.

The next team to get a goal will win the game."

Richard Rabbit and George run off with the football, while everyone is still talking.

"Where's the ball?" asks Peppa.

But it's too late! Richard Rabbit kicks the ball straight into the goal, past Pedro Pony.

"Hooray! The boys win!" cries Danny.

"Football is a silly game," sighs Peppa, disappointed.
"Just a moment," says Daddy Pig. "The boys scored
in their own goal, that means the girls win!"
"Really?" gasp all the girls. "Hooray!"
"Football is a great game!" cheers Peppa.
"Ha, ha, ha!" everyone laughs.